THE PARABLE OF THE GOOD SAMARITAN

"*There was once a man who was going down from Jerusalem to Jericho when robbers attacked him, stripped him, and beat him up, leaving him half dead. It so happened that a priest was going down that road; but when he saw the man, he walked on by, on the other side.*

In the same way a Levite also came along, went over and looked at the man, and then walked on by, on the other side.

But a Samaritan who was travelling that way came upon the man, and when he saw him, his heart was filled with pity. He went over to him, poured oil and wine on his wounds and bandaged them; then he put the man on his own animal and took him to an inn, where he took care of him.

The next day he took out two silver coins and gave them to the innkeeper. 'Take care of him,' he told the innkeeper, 'and when I come back this way, I will pay you whatever else you spend on him.'" St Luke 10, 30-35

Acknowledgment

The above quotation from The Good News Bible *is reproduced by permission of The British and Foreign Bible Society and Collins Publishers.*

The parable of
THE GOOD SAMARITAN

retold for easy reading
by SYLVIA MANDEVILLE
illustrated by DAVID PALMER

Ladybird Books Loughborough

THE GOOD SAMARITAN

Benjamin was sitting up in bed, eating his dinner. He had bandages on his head, and big bruises on his face and arms.

"This food tastes good," he said, smiling at his two children who were sitting by his side. "The food where I have been was all right, but there's nothing like home cooking when you are ill."

"No," said Sarah his wife, "and now you are well enough to talk and eat, we want to hear just where you have been. We have all been so worried about you."

"Yes, please tell us," said the two children, Ruth and James. "What happened to you?"

Benjamin laughed. "Do you really want to hear how I got all these bruises?"

"Yes, please, and the bandages as well," they said.

"Very well, I will tell you," said their father. "As you know, last week I had to take a large sum of money to a friend, down in Jericho.

9

"I was not looking forward to the journey, because there are always too many robbers on the look-out! I thought that if I set off early, there would be plenty of people on the road, and I would be safe.

"It was all right to begin with. I met farmers with their fruit and vegetables for sale, children leading flocks of sheep, and priests coming up to Jerusalem, for the services in the Temple," said Benjamin.

"I had my money well hidden in a bag under my coat, and I wasn't dressed richly, so I hoped that no one would take any notice of me.

"I had been walking for several hours, and the sun was beginning to get hot, when I reached a very narrow part of the road, where the rocks are high on either side. It is always gloomy there, even on the sunniest day."

13

"I know the bit you mean," said Sarah. "It's like a tunnel."

"Yes, that's the bit. No one was in sight as I went further along this road. The last man who had passed me had a load of straw on his back. He was well out of sight."

"I was about half-way through the tunnel when suddenly, there was a shout," their father went on.

"A man jumped on me from behind, and hit me on the head with a stick. I fell to the ground as other men jumped down from where they had been hiding. They ripped my clothes off and snatched my bag.

"They left me half-dead in the road and fled."

"You didn't stand a chance with so many men," said Sarah. "They might have killed you."

"I certainly thought I was dying," said Benjamin. "My face was swollen and bleeding, and my head had a big lump on the back. All my clothes were ripped off."

19

"Where did the robbers go to?" asked James.

"Oh! they ran off quickly to spend the money. I never saw them again."

"What happened next?" said Ruth.

"I think I must have fainted," said Benjamin. "The pains in my head were very bad. I remember wondering if I could drag myself to a more comfortable spot, but when I tried to stand, I was too dizzy."

"Say a Roman chariot with soldiers had come galloping past," said James, "what would you have done? It might have run over you!"

"James, don't say such things," said Sarah, but Benjamin laughed.

"I would have been glad for anyone to come along," he said, "even a Roman chariot! But as I say, I think I fainted just where I was."

Benjamin paused, then went on, "Much later, I heard footsteps. I sat up, groaning with pain. I was so pleased to see a priest coming along. He would help me, I was sure."

"And did he?" asked Ruth.

"No, my dear. When he saw me, groaning and bleeding in the shade of the rocks, he crossed over to the other side of the road, and hurried past."

"But why didn't he help you," said Ruth, "when he should have done?"

"I don't know," said Benjamin. "Perhaps he was in a hurry, or frightened in case the robbers jumped out onto him. What I do know is that he left me and I heard his footsteps hurrying into the distance."

"Didn't you call out after him?" asked Sarah.

"No, I just lay there, and fell asleep. Later, I woke up stiff and aching.

"A man was coming towards me. He was a Levite, one of those good men who help in the Temple. I was sure he would help me. I tried to sit up, but I was too stiff. All I could do was groan," said Benjamin.

"And did he help you?" asked Ruth.

"Perhaps he didn't see me. Perhaps he didn't hear me.

"He crossed over to the other side of the road, just like the priest, and hurried on his way. I lay there listening until I could hear his footsteps no more," said her father.

"How could he have left a
dying man like that?" said
Sarah.

"Did anyone else come along?" said James.

"Yes, another man came by, on a donkey. I took one look at him and gave up hope. I knew that man would never help me."

"Who was it, then? Another robber?" said Ruth.

"No, not a robber, but someone just as bad. It was a foreigner, a Samaritan."

"We never mix with them, do we? They're not good enough," said Ruth.

"No, and we don't talk to them if we can help it," her father answered. "But I have changed my mind about them now, after what happened next."

"Why, what did happen?" said James.

"When the Samaritan saw me, he stopped his little donkey and got off and came over to me," replied Benjamin.

"Full of pity, he knelt by my side and asked me what had happened. I was just able to say the word 'robbers'.

"To my surprise, the Samaritan did not get up and leave me when he heard the word robbers. 'Let me help you,' he said kindly.

"He went over to his donkey, and unpacked some things. Very gently he lifted me into a sitting position. Carefully he bathed my wounds with some wine. It stung, but I knew it would clean them.

"Next, he poured soft olive oil into the wounds and bandaged them up. Although I was in so much pain, I tried to smile at him."

"Then I expect he had to hurry on his way, didn't he?" asked James. "In case the robbers came and got him too?"

"No, he didn't seem to be in any hurry, he took his time and was so gentle. When he had finished bandaging me up, he asked if I could manage to sit on his donkey.

"He helped me to my feet, and with his help, I was just able to get into the saddle."

"He was a good man," said Sarah.

"Yes, he was a good man, and his goodness was not over yet. He walked his donkey very slowly down the road, and held onto me at the same time.

"I knew he would not let me fall off, though several times I was so faint with pain that I thought I would," said Benjamin.

"I cannot remember much of the journey. The next thing I do remember is waking up in bed."

"Where?" asked James.

"It was a bed in a small hotel that stands by the side of the Jericho road. The kind man had taken me there to look after me," Benjamin told them.

"In the morning, he paid the landlord enough money for my keep. 'If it comes to any more than this, I will pay the extra myself when I come past next time,' he told the landlord, and off he went."

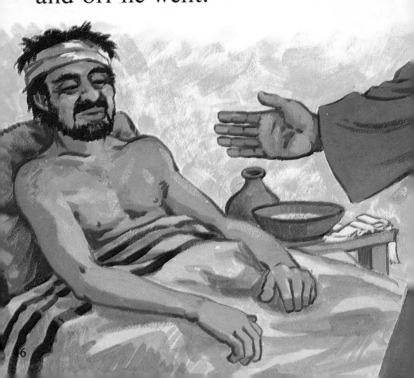

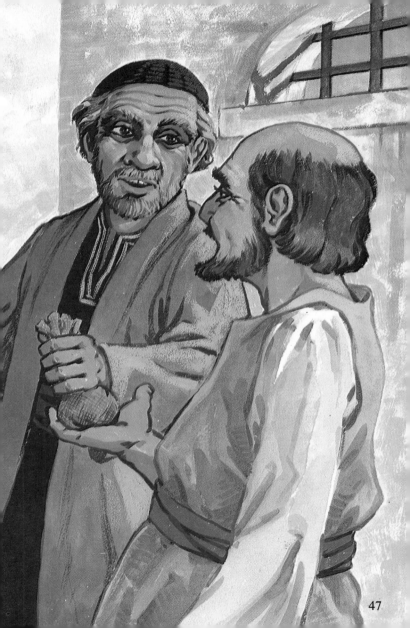

Benjamin smiled at his family. "As soon as I was well enough to get out of bed, I borrowed a donkey from the landlord and hurried home to you all. I knew you would be worrying about me."

"I shall never forget the sight of you as you rode through our gateway," said Sarah, "all bandaged and bruised. How I would like to meet that man and thank him. He saved your life."

"Yes," said Benjamin. "It didn't matter to him that I was a Jew and a foreigner. He saw I needed help, and he looked after me just the same. I shall never forget his kindness all my life."

Jesus told this story to his
friends. He said that if we love
God, we must also love other
people and be kind to them,
just like the Good Samaritan.